Sparky's Excellent Misadventures

My A.D.D. Journal

By Me (Sparky)

written by Phyllis Carpenter and Marti Ford

illustrated by Peter Horjus

MAGINATION PRESS • WASHINGTON, DC

With love to our children Pamela, Philip, Willie, Kate, and Zak,
and a special thanks to Lee Douglass — PC and MF

For my mother and father, my sister Elsa, and my brother Fred
for their love and respect for my funky style — PH

Published by
MAGINATION PRESS
An Educational Publishing Foundation Book
American Psychological Association
750 First Street, NE
Washington, DC 20002

For more information about our books, including a complete catalog,
please write to us, call 1-800-374-2721, or visit our website at
www.maginationpress.com.

Editor: Darcie Conner Johnston
Art Director: Susan K. White
The text type is Kid Script
Printed by Phoenix Color, Rockaway, New Jersey

Library of Congress Cataloging-in-Publication Data

Carpenter, Phyllis.
Sparky's excellent misadventures : my A.D.D. journal (by me. Sparky) /
written by Phyllis Carpenter and Marti Ford ; illustrated by Peter Horjus.
   p. cm.
Summary: A young boy writes in his journal about the frustrations and
triumphs of living with attention deficit disorder.
ISBN 1-55798-606-1
[1. Attention-deficit hyperactivity disorder—Fiction. 2. Diaries—Fiction.]
I. Ford, Marti. II. Horjus, Peter, ill. III. Title.
PZ7.C22646 Sp 1999
[E]—dc21   99-039111
                                                                                          CIP

Manufactured in the United States of America
10 9 8 7 6 5 4 3 2 1

Saturday

Dear Journal,

Hi! My name is Sparky, Spencer Allen Douglass, actually. (I used to forget to put two s's in my last name.) Today is Saturday. I went to Nana's house. I always go to her house on Saturday when Mom works at the bookstore. Nana gave you to me, Journal. She gave me a very shiny red pencil, too.

We looked at old pictures all afternoon. I saw one picture of Grandpa writing in his journal. He was sitting on top of a fire truck at the fire station. Nana says Grandpa had orange hair and "freckers," and his name was Sparky, just like me.

Nana made bread with stuff from her pantry. Her bread smells better than the bread from the store. When it was baking she gave me a big hug.

I didn't pull away 'cause I can tell that Nana needs hugs sometimes. She must get awfully lonely living all by herself. I think she's glad to have me at her house. I really like going to Nana's. I always feel happy, and the itchy feeling in my skin goes away a little.

I bet Spot makes Nana feel not so lonely. Spot is Nana's dog. She found him under her porch one day. She put an ad in the paper to help find his owner, but nobody called. I was glad. Nana let me name him. I picked "Spot" because he has so many. I didn't actually count the spots, but maybe I will next Saturday. Spot likes to sit on me and that helps make my wiggles go away sometimes.

Nana says that I light up her life. I think that is true because her house is always so dark, and the noise is real soft when Mom takes me there. But today when I left, I saw that all of her lights were turned on, and the radio too. I counted eleven lights.

Nana helps me remember things that my brain forgets. She makes up songs with words that sound the same. Stuff like "to remember something new, draw a picture and use words too" and "don't get caught in the trap, write down your assignment like a map."

She says my brain is too smart, and it thinks about everything all at once. My ears hear too much and my eyes see too much. Nana says, "You have eyes like a hawk, little man, and radar ears." She whispers in my ears, some words for one side, and some words for the other. She told me a secret that I am the most special boy in the world. Lots of times Nana says, "I wish that I could borrow just a little bit of your energy." But I worry when I can't control my energy at school.

I'll see you next time, Journal!

Dear Journal,

I am in my room having thinking time. Mom went to buy groceries with Nana. My big brother, Charlie, is in the bathroom getting ready for a "Heather sighting." Heather is the new girl in our neighborhood. Sometimes Charlie pays me a quarter to watch for Heather. We have a big window in our living room, and you can see all kinds of neat stuff going on outside. (Mom likes the window too 'cause she can keep an eye on me when I'm playing.) When I see Heather, I call Charlie and he always finds a reason for going outside. Now that he's in eighth grade, he really likes girls.

I usually go shopping with Mom and Nana, but something happened at church today and I have to be in my room thinking and Charlie gets to be the boss of me. I was trying real hard to sit still in church. I was also trying not to get a "yak attack" in the middle of Pastor William's sermon.

When we sang the first hymn, I used my loudest singing voice. Two ladies even turned around and smiled at me. Charlie was staring at the back of Heather's head way up in front of us, and I started to laugh. Mom gave me one of her looks. I looked down and saw that my shoes weren't tied, so I got on the floor to tie them, and to stop myself from laughing at Charlie. I was quiet the rest of the time.

When church was over and we started to leave, I tripped and fell into a lady. Her extra hair fell almost all the way off, and her regular hair was all flat. Mom's face got red and she made me apologize. Then she noticed that I had tied my shoelaces together.

Charlie laughed. Mom gave him one of her looks. Nana said that it was a calamity. I felt sick to my stomach. Mom sure is a good knot un-doer.
We weren't even the last people out of the church.

I'm hiding in the tent on my bed and I better start thinking before Mom gets home. I want to figure out how to take away the bad things I do. I want everyone to be happy with me. I think it will make Mom happy that I cleaned my room. I didn't put too many things under my bed. I think I really like my shiny red pencil and you, Journal. I think I will put my red pencil in my backpack for school tomorrow. I think I will have a good week at school. That will make my teacher, Mrs. Warren, happy. I think Dad will be home soon from the fire station and that dinner is going to be great.

We are having "bar-B-Q" chicken for dinner tonight. Next to pizza, that's my favorite. I think I will comb my hair and get dressed up for dinner. Mom and Dad are proud when I look clean and handsome. I think I will watch for Heather for free next time. That will make Charlie happy. I think I hear Mom.

Dear Green Paper,
Dad *yelled* at me because
I forgot to put my bike
away last night.

I can't find my journal.

I can't find my red pencil that Nana gave me.

I forgot to bring my library book to school,
even though I almost remember putting it in my
backpack with my red pencil.

I had my shirt on backwards. I bet everybody
thought I was stupid.

I didn't hear Mrs. Warren tell us to write a story,
but I figured it out by myself by looking at the other
kids. She lets me sit in the front row (right next
to her desk) so I won't have an excuse to miss her
instructions. (She told me that when she put me
there.) Anyway, I won't get in trouble 'cause I wrote
a great story. It's called "Nana's House." I want
to write a book someday. Mom loves books.

She said that I should write a story about myself. Charlie said that I have great big ideas, but I'll never sit still long enough to write a book. I bet I get an A on my story. That will show him! And Mrs. Warren will be proud. My story was the only good thing that happened today.

The rest of the day was awful.

I wanted to have the pizza for lunch, so I walked really fast to the lunchroom. Mrs. Pincher said that I was running, and she sent me to the back of the line. The only food left for me was tuna surprise. I HATE tuna surprise. Mrs. Pincher called me "Spencer Allen Douglass" when I was eating the "surprise" stuff. She saw that my foot was kicking the table a lot. Everyone looked at me, and some bigger kids laughed.

I was so happy when I got to go outside to play. I like to run, RUN, RUN, really fast! I think that it helps make the "wild wiggles" go away. But after that, when I found a ball and threw it at the basket, the ball hit Buster Cornwall in the head. I got scared, but I didn't cry. Buster is the biggest, meanest kid at school. His eyes are kind of weird, and his voice sounds scary too. He leaned me back against the wall and called me stupid. That made me so mad I forgot all about being scared, and I hit him! I hit him really hard. Mrs. Pincher made me sit in time out for the rest of recess. She said that I need to start cooperating with her. (But I can't even cooperate with myself.) She said that I would be going to the office the next time I break the rules.

I wanted to tell my side of the story,
but my mouth said, "I hate this school!" I don't
know why I said that. I love my school. Sometimes
I just don't like myself, and I feel so dumb.

I wish I was good at everything, like Charlie.
I wish I was Charlie. He only gets dumb when
he sees Heather.

I hope I find my journal.

Dear Journal,

I found you! I saw a red glow under my bed. It was my very special red pencil. My library book was there, and you were there too! My secret thoughts feel safer when I write them in you, journal, and they won't get holes in them or forgotten right away. I can read my thoughts again and make up ways to get better. I can even write funny things about Charlie and he won't even know. I missed you journal!

When school started, I was shooting pretend aliens with my finger because I didn't know what to do yet, but then Mrs. Warren gave me back my story. She said I had made a good decision to write a story when I didn't have my library book to help me with a book report. But she really liked my story and wrote some ideas on it so that I can fix it a little. She said I can turn it in for extra credit. I still have to do a book report, but that is my only homework because I went to the doctor this afternoon.

Mom said we were just going to talk to Dr. Lee. I'm not sick, and I didn't have to get any shots or anything. Dad met us there. He looked at my story while we waited for Dr. Lee and said my writing is so messy I should be a doctor when I grow up! I like it when Dad makes jokes. He is the best dad!

Anyway, Dr. Lee asked me a lot of questions, and asked Mom a lot of questions, and asked Dad a lot of questions, and read some papers that Mom got from the school office. Dr. Lee said I have an "impish" smile. She said it like it wasn't something wrong, but I'm going to remember to ask Mom if she meant that like a good thing. I didn't like being in that little room for so long, so I went to get a drink of water. The lady at the counter who tells us when to come back again smiled at me and let me choose a sucker.

Guess what color I picked?

That's right! Red!

When we got home, Mom explained that I will be taking some little pills that might help me "focus" at school. Maybe I can do my work like the other kids and not get so far behind. She said that Charlie wears glasses to help his eyes focus in another way. Dad said that everyone has different stuff to learn about themselves, and my stuff is called Attention Deficit Disorder. I copied those big words from this little book the doctor gave me. It explains the big words in kid talk and how my brain does things differently. One thing is that the part of my brain that should tell me to stop doing something doesn't work like it does for most kids. It's kinda like a bike when the brakes don't work the regular way. That doesn't change how smart I am, though.

I have to see Dr. Lee in two weeks to tell her if the pills are helping enough to make my brain work the way it's supposed to. Mom, Dad, and Dr. Lee think that the little pills might help me have better days. I might not have so much homework if I can finish more stuff at school. Then maybe I can play outside on school nights. They really want me to be happy for myself, I think.

Mom said, "We're going to try to help you with your wiggles, but we're going to keep all of your giggles." Then she kissed me. Mom is so nice!

Later, she gave me some neat books she got at her bookstore, Metro Man Saves Planet Z and How to Draw Dogs. I got to have ice cream BEFORE dinner while we waited for the store to put the pills in a bottle. Sometimes Mom gives me pills that can take headaches away. Nana takes pills to stop her shaking hands, and Dad takes pills for his humongous sneezes. I hope that these pills will help my brain work better and fix my wiggles. I didn't know the store made pills to fix MY stuff!

Good-bye, Journal.

Dear Journal,

Hello! Today is Wednesday, and today was the first day for me to take my new pills. I took one at home right after breakfast, and I took one at school right before lunch. I was sort of mad that I had to go get the pill because I was really hungry, but the nurse at school, Miss Karen, is real nice. She gave me real cold water from one of those machines that has a big water bottle on top of it, and the cup looked like a snow cone cup. And besides, there was one boy that plays kick ball with me at recess, and he had to take a pill, too. We walked to the lunchroom together. We weren't even late! I ate all of my lunch and still had time to play outside.

I can't tell if the pills have helped me. Something weird happened though. Someone must have fixed the fan in the ceiling, and they must have fixed the gerbils' running wheel too.

Either that, or Mrs. Warren was trying to talk in her louder voice. I could hear her words a lot better.

Oh, and guess what? This is so cool! Mrs. Warren said that my story is perfect now and she wants to keep it for a while. She even let our principal, Mr. Phillips, read it. Mr. Phillips must have liked it a lot! He told me that if I really try to control my behavior for three weeks, he will buy a pizza for me to share with some other kids at my school. Also, every Friday Mrs. Warren will send me to the office if I have a good week, and Mr. Phillips will let me choose something from his treasure box. (I never knew he had a box with rewards in it!!) Mrs. Warren will give me stickers to show that I am trying my best. I have to try real hard to be good. Mr. Phillips said that this is a "contract"

and contracts are important.
I guess so! Mom and Dad got a
whole entire house with a contract.
I even got to sign my contract.
Mr. Phillips signed it too!
I got a sticker today that says
COOL KID! I'm going to try even harder
tomorrow. I might even try not to write
like a doctor.

When I told Mom about the contract she said
that she believes in me, and that I am very
brave. Don't tell that I said this, but sometimes
Mom kinda worries too much about stuff.
She won't be worried when I get my contract
pizza! I'm going to ask for extra cheese! Charlie
will be jealous of me. For one time Charlie will
wish he was me! This is just so great! This is
the best day of my life!

Adios, Journal!

Thursday

Dear Journal,

We had an important visitor in our class today. Her name is Mrs. Saunders. She's our school's brand new counselor. Our old counselor was Ms. Clews. She moved to North Dakota, where it is really C-O-L-D!! She showed me pictures of all the snow. I miss her. I used to go to her office on some Thursdays, and she would let me talk about some bad feelings I have sometimes, like when I mess up on my school work, or when I have trouble at recess. Sometimes it's easier to talk about feelings when Mom and Dad aren't there. She helped me understand about problems and how to fix them. She told me to walk away from a kid who is making bad decisions and tell a teacher if someone is really bothering me.

Anyway, Mrs. Saunders is so nice and really pretty! I think she's even prettier than Heather.

She talks kinda funny. When she came in she said, "Hi, y'all."

She does neat things to make us pay attention. She said, "All eyes on me!" I thought of a bunch of big eyes glued on her yellow dress and I laughed (just a little). Mrs. Saunders winked at me.

A couple of times when she walked by my desk she put her hand on my shoulder. At first I thought that I was doing something wrong, but then I figured out that she was probably understanding me. She also does this cool thing called think time. She asks a question, then counts to 10 in her head so everybody can think about what their best answer will be. It helped me to not yell out an answer right away, like I sometimes do in class by mistake.

We got to give our ideas about how the whole class could work together, kinda like a family. My idea was to say kind words to each other. Mrs. Saunders wrote our ideas on the chalkboard. She used different colors of chalk.

When Mrs. Saunders was talking to us, Mrs. Warren sat at one of the kid desks and wrote some ideas in a little book. I pretended that she was a student like us. I never thought about my teacher having to learn stuff before. That seems too weird!

After lunch, Mrs. Warren let me do a special job. I took Willie Martin's homework up to the office for his mom to pick up. He is sick at home with chicken pox. I always feel better when I can walk. It's hard to sit at my desk for a long time. I think that my feet would go for a walk without me if they could. I can tell the little pills help a lot, but I still have some extra energy. Dr. Lee told me that even though I take the pills, I also have to try the ideas that my counselor told me about. Mom and Dad and I practice the ideas at home. Charlie wants to pretend to be mean to me to help me practice, but Mom says that probably isn't a good idea.

On my way back to class, I saw Mrs. Saunders. She let me see her office. She has a really cool office! There are dragons everywhere! I counted 30 dragon things. I didn't know that grown-ups had fun things at their work. My favorite is the dragon stapler. It's kinda like the dragon bites the papers.

Mrs. Saunders told me a secret. She and I have the same Attention Deficit Disorder stuff about ourselves. She just calls it by initials. A.D.D. I couldn't believe it! She is so smart! Even Mrs.

Warren wanted to learn from her.
She told me that lots of people with
A.D.D. are good at many things. A lot
of artists, actors, writers, and other
really important people have A.D.D. Some
of the people are Tom Clayton the baseball player,
Kate Michaels the rock star, and even Zak Jones,
the guy who writes Metro Man books! Mrs. Saunders
said that I should be proud of some of my qualities,
and work to control the things that get me in
trouble at school. She said that I get to come
talk to her on Thursdays, just like I talked to
Ms. Clews. She said that she is sure that we will
become good friends. I've never had a grown-up
friend before. This might be cool!

I got a sticker today, but it was kinda small.
Mrs. Warren said that I had a good day, except
for the part when I spit water on Christine at the
drinking fountain during recess. It was an accident,
sort of. Christine kept bugging me to hurry up.

When I was done, I said, OK, I'M DONE NOW!
and some water came out of my mouth. It got on
Christine's shirt. Mrs. Warren told me she is sure
that I will make better decisions tomorrow. I will try
to keep the water in my mouth. I hope Christine will
keep her words in her mouth!

Hey, Journal, I got tired of writing, but I'm back now.

Mom ordered a PIZZA for dinner tonight. She said
that it was just because. I am *really* glad that I
can eat *regular* food again. Last summer Mom
and Dad read a book about healthy food for kids.
They thought me eating some different food would
take some of my extra energy away, but it didn't
help me. We eat most of our regular food
again now, but I promised Mom and Dad
I would eat healthy breakfasts and snacks.
I really like grapes. I like to see how high
I can toss them and then catch them in my
mouth. (Mom says I have to do that outside.)

Pretzels are okay too. You can lean them against each other and build cool things.

Anyway, after dinner I told Mom, Dad, and Charlie about the famous people who have what I have. We guessed that Tim Perry, the funny actor, has A.D.D. We laughed a lot tonight. Something strange is happening to my life. Even Charlie was nice to me ALL night. This is great!

Tomorrow is Friday. Every Friday a dad or mom can come to our class to tell us about the job they do. Dad is coming to my class tomorrow. It's treasure chest day too! I think I'm feeling better about going to school.

Good Bye

Good-bye, friend Journal!

Hiya, Journal!

First... some bad news:

This morning at school everybody got a different place to sit. I'm still at the front of the room, but now I'm right in the middle. I am right where Mrs. Warren stands when she talks to the class, AND I have to sit next to Courtney Lewis. She's pretty quiet and she seems OK for a girl, but she's too good at knowing the right answers. Sometimes I worry so much about being called on that I can't give Mrs. Warren any answer, not even a wrong answer, because I forget the question! Anyway, I can't sit with Willie anymore 'cause now he'll be way at the back of the room when he gets back from the chicken pox. We used to have fun when no one was looking. At least I'll get to call Willie after school if I forget what my homework is. Mrs. Warren said so.

Now, some good news:

We probably got moved because Mrs. Warren needed to make room for another desk. We have a new boy in our class. His name is Darren. I met him before school. He was standing in our line looking kinda scared, so I talked to him. I told him we have the best class in the whole entire school! Mrs. Warren let me be his special pal today. I helped him find his desk. I even let him use my shiny red pencil. He said all of his school stuff is still packed. The only things he brought to school were lunch money and a pair of broken glasses. (One of the sides is missing.) I bet he wears glasses all the time, because when he looks at me he squinches his face. I tried to imagine what it would be like if I couldn't see everything. I hope Darren gets new glasses real soon.

Now I have some great news!

When Dad came to school today, he brought a

new, *really* cool video about fire safety. And he even brought his special fireman's suit. Mrs. Warren tried it on and she looked funny! We all laughed so hard! All the kids liked my dad, just as much as they liked Joseph's mom, Police Officer Erica! I was so proud!

Now I have some REALLY great news!

A man from a radio station called Mr. Phillips and wants to have some kids read their own stories on the radio. Mr. Phillips remembered my story and told Mrs. Warren he wants me to be one of the kids! Mr. Phillips gave me a *really* important special writing award. It has a gold circle on it! Mrs. Warren gave me a big hug.

Her eyes looked kinda watery, and a tear leaked out. I asked her if she was sad 'cause she never had an award like mine. I didn't want her to feel sad. She said that she was happy and proud.

She whispered in my ear that I am a treasure and I have made her a better teacher.

I got a GIANT sticker for being in control today. I even used friendly words and not my hands when a big kid crashed into me in the lunch line. He looked at me kinda confused, like he didn't think I would act OK like that, and then he even said "sorry." When I went to the treasure box I could pick two things. I picked a super bouncy ball for me and a pencil for Darren. It has Metro Man on it.

Well, Journal, dinner is almost ready, so I better stop writing. Mom and Dad are fixing tacos (my third favorite!).

Charlie is in the bathroom putting goo in his hair and using some of Dad's favorite foo-foo water. (He hopes to see You-Know-Who later.)

My whole family was excited about my day today. Mom's going to put my award in a frame and hang it near Charlie's football trophy. Charlie said he wants to be on the radio someday. He said I'm pretty OK for a little brother!

I bet Nana will be happy tomorrow when I tell her about my award. Mom wanted to tell her when they talked on the phone, but I said I wanted to surprise her. Nana and I will have lots to talk about. I might not even have time to count the spots on Spot!

This is the bestest day any kid ever had!
This was even a pretty great week.
I don't want to, but I'd better stop writing,
at least for now.
This is Spencer Allen Douglass, author, signing off!

Oh yeah, I almost forgot.
This is what my award
looks like!

Sparky